Magical ♡ Rescue Vets

Holly the Flying Horse

Melody Lockhart

Books in the Magical Rescue Vets series

Oona the Unicorn
Jade the Gem Dragon
Blaze the Phoenix
Holly the Flying Horse

This edition published in 2022 by Arcturus Publishing Limited
26/27 Bickels Yard, 151–153 Bermondsey Street,
London SE1 3HA

Author: Melody Lockhart
Illustrator: Morgan Huff
Story editor: Xanna Eve Chown
Project editor: Joe Harris
Designers: Jeni Child and Rosie Bellwood

CH008345NT
Supplier 10, Date 0422, Print run 00000578

Printed in the UK

Contents

Chapter 1
The New Girl

It was perfect, Kat thought. The school holidays were finally here, and Springhaven was covered in snow! She smiled to herself as she worked to clear the yard around the henhouse at the bottom of her garden. She couldn't wait to spend the winter break with her family—and their many pets—in their little house at the edge of Starfall Forest.

"We love winter," yelled her little brothers, Jorden and Jayden, flipping snow at each other with their spades and giggling.

"It's a shame Mrs. Cluckington and the other chickens don't agree," laughed Dad.

Just then, Kat noticed something fluttering in one of the frozen flowerbeds. Had one of the chickens escaped? She took a closer look and gasped. It wasn't a chicken—it was a little book, flapping its pages as if they were wings!

Very gently, Kat scooped up the book and examined the cover. The picture showed a pretty fountain covered in carvings of smiling mermaids and winged horses.

It reminded her of the one in her best friend Rosie's garden. Rosie lived in Willow Cottage, right next door to Starfall Forest. The forest was home to Calico Comfrey's Veterinary Surgery, a very special place that took care of all the magical creatures that lived there. Rosie and Kat adored animals—from dogs to dragons—and loved to help out whenever they got a chance.

Suddenly, the book gave a shiver. The poor thing must be freezing! Carefully, Kat tucked it into her warm pocket. She couldn't wait to tell Rosie! They'd been best friends ever since Rosie moved to Springhaven, and life was much more fun when she was around. Kat loved having someone to share secrets with—secrets like the magical book that was now snoring gently in her pocket ...

Kat rushed back into the house and nearly collided with her mother, who was coming in the front door, carrying her baby sister Brianna and two shopping bags. Kat stopped to give Brianna a big squeezy hug and the little girl burbled in pleasure.

"Mama's home!" shouted the twins, rushing and bumping into the room to say hello. Kat grinned. Her family was large and chaotic but she wouldn't change it for the world.

"Mama, can I go to Rosie's house?" Kat asked. "I've got something to show her."

"You won't find her at home," smiled her mother. "I just saw her at the playground."

"Even better!" said Kat. She slipped on her boots again and dashed outside ... But she was in for a shock. Rosie was at the playground, hard at work building a snowman with another girl. Someone Kat didn't know.

"Kat! Hi!" called Rosie, waving at her friend. "Come and meet Lunella."

Kat suddenly felt a bit awkward. Now she couldn't show Rosie the book! No one else knew about the magic of Starfall Forest and it was important for it to stay that way. It was a safe haven for magical creatures, who could live there peacefully, knowing they wouldn't be disturbed.

"Hi Kat," said Lunella. She had long dark hair and a cute winter hat pulled down over her ears. "There's someone else who'd like to meet you," she said, pointing to the snowman. Then she put on a silly, rumbly voice and said, "Helloooooo! I'm Mr. Freezy and I just rode here on my icicle-bicycle!"

Kat couldn't help smiling. "I've not seen you in Springhaven before," she said. "Do you live nearby?"

"We, er, move around a lot," said Lunella, biting her lip and looking away.

Kat's eyes were drawn to Lunella's sparkly pendant. "That's really pretty," she said.

"Thanks," beamed Lunella. "It was a gift from my fairy godmother!"

Rosie burst into fits of giggles. "Lunella's so funny," she said. "Hey, show Kat that special whistle you can do!" Lunella crossed her eyes and pursed her lips. Then she whistled two notes at once, one low and one high. It sounded amazing! Kat tried to copy her but she couldn't even whistle one! Lunella  offered to teach her, but Kat shook her head. She didn't want to learn how to whistle—she wanted to show Rosie the book!

"Shall we finish Mr. Freezy?" Lunella asked, then put on the funny voice again. "It would be *snow* good to have more decoration."

"Sorry, we can't," said Kat quickly. "Rosie and I have to go and do that ... thing." Rosie looked puzzled. "You know," said Kat, waggling her eyebrows. "In Starfall Forest?"

"Oh," said Rosie. "*That* thing. Sorry, Lunella. Let's meet up tomorrow in the café for that hot chocolate!" Kat's stomach did an unexpected flip. The café was her and Rosie's special place!

"Sounds great," said Lunella cheerfully. "Oh, before you go … You haven't seen any horses around here recently, have you?" What a strange question, Kat thought, shaking her head. Lunella's face fell. "Well, if you do, can you let me know? I love animals."

"Okay," Kat said—breathing a huge sigh of relief as they left the playground.

"Isn't Lunella great?" Rosie said, her eyes sparkling. "She's so much fun. Should we tell her about the animals in Starfall Forest—and the vets? She'd be so excited!"

"What? No!" Kat was astonished that Rosie had even suggested it. There was an enchantment on the forest which protected the magical animals that lived there. If anyone tried to enter, they would suddenly think of somewhere else they had to be! It didn't affect Rosie because she lived in Willow Cottage, an old house that had once belonged to the famous wizard, Calico Comfrey. At first, Kat hadn't believed Rosie's stories about the forest—then her friend showed her the secret way in at the bottom of her garden ...

Kat waited until they were in Rosie's overgrown garden before showing her the book.

"*Magical Fountains and Wells …* " Rosie read. She took it in her hands and carefully flicked through the pages. "It mentions *our* fountain!" she said, pointing excitedly at a picture. "It says here that if you shut your eyes and wish hard enough, it will show you a vision of the future." She snapped the book shut and handed it back to Kat. "We *have* to try it out!"

The noise seemed to make the magic book wake up. It gave a little wriggle, then fluttered sleepily out of Kat's hands and perched on a pile of snow-covered leaves.

Suddenly there was a sound like a tuba being played. *Hooonnnkkkk!* A purple, toad-like creature with pink horns stuck

its head out of the leaves and
them. The book whooshed up i
in alarm and began flapping a
girls' heads.

"Don't worry, it's only a groak," said
Rosie. "They like to sleep in the leaves to
keep warm!"

The book looped around their heads,
then began to flutter away through the
frosty trees.

"I bet it's heading for the fountain," said
Kat. "Let's follow it!"

The fountain looked more magical than ever with sparkling icicles dripping around the bowl. The water was mostly frozen over, but there was a hole in the ice, and Kat could see flashes of silver as fish darted about beneath it.

She squeezed her eyes shut and held tightly onto the rim of the fountain. "I wish to see the future," she whispered.

When she opened her eyes, the water had changed from dark green to sky blue. A beautiful brown horse galloped into view, with a soft white mane, long lashes, and enormous feathery white wings.

"We're going to meet a flying horse," breathed Kat.

"It's better than that," said Rosie, her eyes widening. "We're going to *ride* one."

Sure enough, when Kat took a close look, there were two figures sitting on the horse's back. She couldn't help feeling secretly pleased that Lunella was nowhere to be seen! The picture faded, and the girls looked at each other in excitement. When would they ride the flying horse?

"I hope it's soon," said Rosie dreamily, as the girls made their way through the old gate that led into the snowy forest.

Chapter 2
The Flying Library

The book perched on Kat's shoulder as she pushed the lump of bark on the oak tree that revealed the secret entrance to the surgery.

To their surprise, Doctor Hart was standing on the spiral staircase just inside the tree. The kindly lady was the head vet at the surgery. "Stop the flutterpuff!" she exclaimed, as a yellow ball of fuzz with tiny wings bounced toward the girls.

Kat grabbed hold of the little creature and held it tight. It wriggled and giggled in her arms and—*Pop!*—another flutterpuff suddenly appeared under Doctor Hart's hat.

With a sigh, the vet handed the flutterpuff to Rosie. Now both girls had one! They carried the creatures down the tunnel to the surgery and found it full of flutterpuffs too.

"No! No! No! Don't let them out!" A funny tree-stump creature with a green moss-tache quickly shut the door behind them. This was Quibble, the surgery porter.

A heap of flutterpuffs beside him shook and tumbled away to reveal the tiny figure of Doctor Morel. "Oh my spoons and jars!" said the gnome. "This is a disaster!"

"One of the flutterpuffs has caught copypox," explained Doctor Hart. "Whenever it giggles, another one appears." *Pop!* Right on cue, another flutterpuff appeared under her large, flowery hat.

"That sounds great!" said Rosie, who adored the little fluffy animals.

Doctor Hart shook her head. "It's very serious," she said. "Copypox is catching. Soon the whole surgery will fill up with flutterpuffs … then the forest … then all of Springhaven! Luckily, there's a potion that can cure it. I'm just on my way to the flying library to find the recipe." She looked at the book on Kat's shoulder. "Do you girls want to come with me?" she asked. "It looks like you've got a book to return."

The girls exchanged an excited glance. They had never heard of the flying library before. Eagerly, they followed Doctor Hart to an enormous room filled with books of all shapes and sizes. They were nesting on the tall bookshelves, swooping around the ceiling, and dozing on the windowsills. The little book left Kat's shoulder and flew to a warm spot by the fire.

"Books from the flying library make their own way home when you've finished reading them," said Doctor Hart. "This little one must have gotten lost."

Doctor Hart fetched the girls a pair of sparkly butterfly nets. "We need to find a book called *Happy Herbology*," she told them. "It's big and green with stars and daisies on the cover."

Kat and Rosie started to search the library. It was lots of fun, and soon the girls were breathless from running and giggling. Every time she saw a large, green book, Kat swooshed her net to catch it—only to let it go again when it turned out

to be the wrong one. She was sure that a playful book called *Magical Cupcakes* kept flying into her net on purpose!

At last, Kat spotted the book they were looking for at the top of a very tall shelf.

"Whistle and it will come to you," said Doctor Hart.

But Kat couldn't whistle, so she climbed up the wobbly ladder to reach it instead.

"Be careful!" warned Rosie as Kat grabbed the book and began to climb back down. "I wish Lunella was here," she added. "She's great at whistling!"

For a moment, Kat's heart sank. Then she spotted a book with a flying horse on the cover. Never mind, she thought. She still had that ride on a flying horse with her best friend to look forward to. Nothing—and no one—would ever come between them!

Doctor Hart found the recipe she was looking for and ran her finger down the list of ingredients. "Singing nettles ... Sparkleberries ... Bubblegum blossom." she read, then frowned. "I've got everything except the last one. I think it grows in the Lollipop Orchard."

Kat was sure she'd seen the sticky pink flowers before. "We'll get you some," she said.

"That's a great idea," beamed Doctor Hart. "But you'll need to be quick! Doctor Clarice can give you a lift on the flying carpet."

Doctor Clarice was tinkering in her lab— as usual! She loved inventing amazing machines for the surgery. She put down her tools when she saw the girls. "I've just finished adding a heated layer to the carpet," she said excitedly, pushing her glasses up

her nose. "It will be a really warm ride. No more cold behinds *this* winter!"

The girls hopped on, and Doctor Clarice steered the flying carpet out of the room in a stream of rainbow bubbles. Up, up, up they went until they were soaring over the snowy forest, which glittered far below. Kat was dazzled by the beautiful sight—and she could tell that Rosie was feeling exactly the same way.

The carpet reached the Lollipop Orchard and landed with a bump in the powdery snow, scattering a family of squeaking sugar mice. There was a sweet smell in the air, and you could almost taste the candy on the breeze. In the distance, a grouchy gummy bear poked its head out of its cave and gave a wobbly roar.

"These banana-split trees have given me an idea," said Doctor Clarice. "Let's *split* up to search for the blossom. It will be quicker!"

The girls agreed, but they hadn't gone far when they heard a soft whizzing noise coming from Kat's pocket. "My crystalzoometer!" said Kat. She took out the magical locket and saw the crystal inside spinning frantically. "There must be an injured animal nearby."

"Let's find Doctor Clarice," said Rosie— but Kat was already racing through the snow.

"There's no need," Kat called over her shoulder. "Doctor Hart wouldn't have given us our own crystalzoometers if she didn't trust us to use them … Urgh!" She suddenly found that she was up to her knees in a chocolate toffee bog. "Help!" she called. "I'm stuck."

"Hang on!" Rosie called. She reached out her hand to help her friend but lost her balance and slipped into the bog beside her with a loud squelch …

The girls felt very sorry for themselves as they stumbled out of the bog. Kat opened up her crystalzoometer and groaned. The crystal wasn't glowing or quivering anymore because it was covered in a thick layer of sticky, brown gloop.

"Mine's just as bad," Rosie groaned. "How are we going to find the hurt animal now?"

Just then, they saw a very strange sight. A group of gingerbread people had gathered at the edge of the bog and they were all shouting in squeaky voices.

"What are they saying?" whispered Rosie. "I don't speak Gingerbread!"

"I don't either," Kat whispered back. "But that one looks like he's in charge!"

One of the gingerbread men stepped forward. He was wearing a mayor's hat, trimmed with piped white icing, and had a white-icing chain around his neck. He clapped his hands together until the gingerbread folk had quietened down, then pointed to the trees on the side of the orchard.

"I think he wants to show us something," said Kat. She nodded to the little man to show that she understood and started to squelch after him. Her boots were full of gooey chocolate toffee.

Kat and Rosie soon forgot about their sticky clothes when they saw what the mayor wanted to show them. At the edge of the orchard, there was a beautiful horse with feathery white wings ... caught in a thick rope.

"That's the horse we saw in the fountain," said Rosie in a hushed voice.

As they got closer, they could see that

the rope was caught in a frosty holly bush. The more the poor horse struggled, the more tangled she got. She looked up at the girls and gave a sad whinny. Kat could tell that she was tired and afraid.

They approached her slowly. "Don't be scared," said Rosie in a slow, calm voice. She held out a hand and gently stroked the horse's soft nose. "We're here to help."

The horse leaned forward and licked some of the sticky toffee from the girl's hair. Rosie laughed and the horse gave a happy-sounding snort.

"She really likes you," said Kat. "Let's call her Holly—because she's stuck in a holly bush! Don't worry, Holly. We are going to get you out of this mess!" She examined the rope and tried to pull it off the bush, but it was no use. Holly was really stuck!

Chapter 3
Fixing the Flutterpuffs

*W*hen Doctor Clarice arrived with a basket full of bubblegum blossoms, she was surprised at the girls' sticky appearance. She was even more surprised to see Holly!

Rosie stroked Holly's nose while Doctor Clarice inspected the rope. She looked very serious. "This isn't just any old rope," she said. "It's covered in enchantments. Luckily, I never go anywhere without a pair of magical scissors." She took out a pair of long-handled silver scissors and snipped at the air. At once, the scissors wobbled out of her hands and hovered above the holly bush.

"They're very special scissors," she explained to the girls as they snip-snipped at the air above the ropes. "They can cut any kind of rope or net—even ones that are laced with magic like this one—but they can never harm a living thing."

Holly seemed to know what was happening. She stayed still while the scissors worked busily away, but when she was finally free, she made no move to fly away.

Doctor Clarice checked her over. "I think the rope has damaged her wing," she said. "We'd better get her back to the surgery."

The gingerbread mayor waved his little arms around. He was extremely glad that Holly was safe and shouted in his squeaky voice until the rest of the gingerbread folk came to look. They tumbled out of their gingerbread cottages and crowded around, chattering loudly. Kat couldn't

understand a word—but she could tell that they were pleased. Two little gingerbread children ran over with a basket of pink and white striped candy canes, which the mayor presented to the girls.

"Oh my goodness," said Doctor Clarice. "An everlasting basket of candy canes. What a wonderful gift! No matter how many you eat, the basket will always be full."

Kat's eyes widened and she thanked the gingerbread people very much. Then she and Rosie took a tiny candy cane each and popped them into their mouths. Delicious!

"Now we'd better get going," said Doctor Clarice. "Holly needs attention—and I think that you two need a bath." She took a silver whistle from her coat pocket and blew three times. In a moment, the magic carpet flew toward them like an obedient puppy.

Kat helped Holly settle on the flying carpet and she neighed softly, pleased to be somewhere warm and comfortable. Rosie wrapped her scarf around Holly's neck, and the horse nuzzled her neck in appreciation. "I know you'll be well enough to fly again," Rosie said. "I've seen it in the magic fountain!"

Doctor Clarice steered the carpet up into

the sky and the cold wind whipped at Holly's white mane. Kat stroked the horse's soft flanks. "I wonder how she got tangled up in that net," she said.

"I've been wondering that too," said Doctor Clarice. "I'm afraid that I don't think it was an accident."

"What?" gasped Rosie. "Who would want to hurt such a beautiful animal?"

"Poachers," said Doctor Clarice sadly. "People who travel to Starfall Forest to steal the magical animals."

Kat and Rosie exchanged worried glances.

"I'll have to tell Doctor Hart about my suspicions," said Doctor Clarice. "Then we can go back to the Lollipop Orchard tomorrow and look for clues. I'd like to find out who these poachers are!"

As the flying carpet approached the surgery, Kat heard a funny giggling noise. In all the excitement, she had almost forgotten about the flutterpuffs! It sounded like a lot more had popped up while they'd been away.

"It sounds like there's no time to lose," said Doctor Clarice. She reached into her basket and pulled out a handful of sticky bubblegum blossoms. "Now, if I remember the recipe correctly, these need to be torn into tiny pieces for the potion to be a success. Kat, can you fly the carpet while I work?"

"I think so," said Kat nervously.

"Just listen to the hum of the engine," said Doctor Clarice. "When you can really feel that hum in your mind, you're ready! Think about the direction you want to go and the carpet will follow."

Kat closed her eyes and concentrated on the hum, stroking the carpet with her fingertips. "Turn left," she thought and, to her delight, the carpet made a smooth turn. She could hardly believe it! "Turn right," she thought—and the carpet moved just like she wanted. She was really doing it!

"You're really good at this," said Rosie, and Kat beamed proudly.

Doctor Clarice finished tearing up the blossoms as Kat steered the carpet in to land. She gave the girls the basket and led Holly away to examine her wing. The corridors were stuffed with jostling flutterpuffs, and the girls had to push their way past mounds of the fluffy creatures to get through.

Doctor Hart was very pleased that the blossoms had already been torn. "That saves us some time," she said, mixing them into her potion right away. "All the flutterpuffs need a dose, just to be safe." But when she offered a spoonful of the pink, gloopy liquid to the nearest creature, it wrinkled up its nose and skittered away. In fact, not a single flutterpuff would taste even the tiniest drop. "This is hopeless," she sighed.

Fixing the Flutterpuffs

Then, Kat had an idea. They could use the everlasting basket of candy canes! Doctor Hart thought this was an excellent plan, so they set to work dipping them in the potion and handing them out to the flutterpuffs. One by one, all the little creatures took a tasty treat, then fluttered off into the snowy forest, licking their lips happily.

Chapter 4
Kat's Secret

The next day, Kat walked very slowly to the café. She usually raced all the way to meet Rosie, but it didn't feel as special knowing that someone else would be there too.

Both Rosie and Lunella had steaming mugs of hot chocolate in front of them already.

"I've never had hot chocolate before,"

Lunella said. "It tastes so good! We got extra cream and toffee sauce. Do you want to try?"

Kat shook her head. She couldn't believe that they had ordered their drinks without her. The toffee sauce made her think of the sticky bog in the Lollipop Orchard, and her stomach gave an unpleasant lurch.

"I've brought some things from my garden to decorate Mr. Freezy," Lunella said. She reached into her bag and pulled out a handful of rainbow stones and sparkly white feathers. They seemed perfect for decorating a snowman—but they hadn't come from any kind of garden Kat had ever seen.

"Where do you live again?" she asked.

"With my father," said Lunella. "He's … away at the moment." She paused. "You didn't see any horses in the forest yesterday, did you?"

Rosie broke into a huge smile. "We did," she said. Kat shot her a warning look, but it was too late. "She had wings!" Rosie added.

Kat waited for Lunella to laugh, but instead, the girl looked very interested. "A flying horse?" she said. "How wonderful!"

"She was beautiful," gushed Rosie. "But she'd hurt her wing. It's lucky that ... Ouch!"

Kat had kicked Rosie's ankle under the table hard to shut her up. "She's joking," Kat said quickly. "We pretend there are magical creatures in the woods—it's a game."

Rosie rubbed her ankle. It was clear that she didn't know what to say. "Let's all go and decorate Mr. Freezy," she said eventually.

"I'll stay here," said Kat. "After all, he's *your* snowman."

Rosie looked confused and a little hurt.

"We won't be long," said Lunella. "My dad

worries if I get home too late." That's strange, Kat thought. Hadn't she just said that her father was away?

Kat watched as Rosie and Lunella picked up the feathers and stones and left the café. Now she was all on her own, she didn't like it. She could see Rosie and Lunella through the window, catching snowflakes on their tongues, and started to feel sorry that she'd stayed behind. It would have been nice to stick glittering stones on Mr. Freezy.

Suddenly, Kat noticed that Lunella had left her bag hanging on her chair. There was a pretty blue journal peeking out of the top. Without really thinking, Kat reached across to take a look.

As she pulled the journal out of Lunella's bag, a drawing fell out and fluttered to the floor. Kat reached down and picked it up.

It was a picture of a horse. But not just any horse … A horse with beautiful, feathery wings. It had to be Holly! Kat gasped as she took a closer look. Yes, Lunella's drawing had the same soft white wings, silky mane, and long eyelashes. There was no way this was a coincidence!

Kat's mind started to race. She remembered how calm Lunella had been when Rosie mentioned a horse with wings. In fact, she hadn't seemed surprised at all. Lunella must have met Holly … But how?

Kat looked up and saw Lunella and Rosie heading back to the café. Before she knew what she was doing, Kat quickly stuffed the journal and the picture into her own bag. Her cheeks were burning with a mixture of excitement and fear—but it was too late to change her mind.

Kat and Rosie said goodbye to Lunella, then set off through the snow to the surgery. All the way there, Rosie chattered happily about Lunella and the snowman, but Kat was hardly listening. The more she thought about what she'd done, the worse she felt. She wanted to show Rosie the drawing— but she couldn't do that without admitting that she'd stolen it! I'll wait until we get to the surgery, she thought. Then I'll explain what I've done ...

But when the girls reached the old oak tree, there was no time to talk. The surgery was busier than Kat had ever seen it before! Worried gnomes had been bringing in animals for the vets to examine all day from all the corners of Starfall Forest. Some were tangled in ropes, others were exhausted and scared after escaping from nets and traps.

"So, it's not just flying horses that the poachers are interested in," said Kat sadly.

"Oh my boots and buttons!" said Doctor Morel. "I'm glad to see you two. We need all the help we can get today." He was hard at work untangling a round, feathery cahoot from a long rope. Beside him were two baby grufflegoats whose wool had turned bright red with alarm. "Doctor Clarice has gone out with her crystalzoometer," he added. "It hasn't stopped buzzing all day!"

Kat and Rosie went to find Doctor Hart, who was looking after Holly. The little horse neighed happily to see them.

"You'll be pleased to know that her wing is almost as good as new," said Doctor Hart. "Flying horses heal very quickly, but ... I don't think Holly is ready to leave just yet. She's had a nasty fright and is too scared to be left on her own."

Kat felt very sorry for poor Holly and asked what she could do to help.

"I'm sure she wouldn't say no to a snack," said Doctor Hart with a twinkle in her eye.

Kat fed Holly a crunchy carrot, and Doctor Hart showed Rosie where the brushes and ribbons were kept. Rosie brushed Holly's soft coat until it shone, then braided her mane and tail and tied the ends in a beautiful bow. When it was done, Doctor Hart said Holly needed to rest. She asked the girls if they wanted to help with the grufflegoats, but Kat shook her head.

"You go without me," said Kat. "There's something I want to do first."

"Okay," said Rosie, looking surprised.

Kat's heart pounded as she hurried along the corridor to the flying library. Inside, Quibble was busily tidying up the bookshelves with a dustpan and brush.

"My, my, my, what a mess these baby booklets make," he said. "Especially when they are learning to fly."

Kat found a quiet spot and took out the journal. Her heart was still thumping in her chest. There's no turning back now, she told herself sternly. She *had* to find out why Lunella had been drawing pictures of Holly. But, when she opened the book, she found that she couldn't understand a single word. Was it written in some kind of code?

She decided to show the journal to Quibble, who was tidying up the books' nests in the Magical Romance section of the library. Perhaps he would be able to help.

The little tree-stump man examined the spidery writing for a moment then flapped his twiglike arms up and down. "Yes, yes, yes, that's Elf language," he said in his high pitched voice. "I'll find you a dictionary." And he skittered off, leaving Kat staring at the page in shock. Could Lunella really be an elf?

It wasn't easy to read Lunella's journal, even with the help of Quibble's elf dictionary, but there was one phrase that appeared over and over again: "The Elf King."

"Dreadful, dreadful, dreadful!" spluttered Quibble when Kat mentioned it to him. "That man is not a friend to animals or plantfolk." He told her that the Elf King

lived in Cloud Castle, which flew around the world looking for magical creatures to put in his private zoo. The zoo was guarded day and night, and no one was allowed in to see the animals except him. "He sends out special animal collectors," said Quibble, his green moss-tache quivering in indignation. "They find the rarest magical animals for him."

Kat had a sudden, awful thought. What if *Lunella* was one of the Elf King's animal collectors? She could have been sent out to find him a flying horse! It would certainly explain why she kept asking if they had seen any horses—and why she had been making drawings of Holly. Perhaps ... Kat shivered ... Perhaps, she was the one who had tried to catch Holly and hurt her poor wing!

Kat snapped the journal shut and shoved it back in her bag. What was she going to *do*? She wanted to tell Rosie what she had discovered—but it was impossible. The longer she left it, the worse it got. She had taken Lunella's journal and read it. Rosie would be so shocked. What would she say? It was all too awful to imagine.

Kat felt very miserable. She thanked Quibble for his help and headed back to the surgery. She found Rosie snuggled up on a beanbag with the two little grufflegoats. Their wool had changed from angry red to a much happier yellow.

"Hey, Kat! Listen to this," she said. She stood up and a pretty bird with a long droopy tail flew down and perched on her arm. "Say hello to Kat," she instructed.

"Yas olleh ot Tak!" chirped the bird, and Rosie burst out laughing.

"It's a back-to-front bird," she said. 'It repeats anything you say—only backward!"

"Drawkcab!" agreed the bird. Kat tried to smile, but her heart wasn't in it.

"I wish we could have brought Lunella with us," said Rosie with a sigh. "She'd think this was so funny!"

"Allenul! Allenul!" chirruped the bird.

That evening, Kat's mother made one of the meals that Kat liked best in the world—sweet potato pie. But Kat wasn't hungry. She pushed the food around her plate with her fork without tasting it. She didn't even laugh when baby Brianna splatted her food with a spoon and got mushed-up peas all around her mouth.

"I'm thinking of getting some new hens for the yard," said her father. "Does anyone have any good ideas for their names?" Usually, Kat would have lots of ideas, but today she just shrugged.

"Henny and Penny!" yelled Jordan.

"No!" shouted Jayden. "Spotty and Dotty!"

"No! Henny and Penny!" shouted Jordan again. He flicked a piece of pie at his twin, who started to yell.

"That's enough!" said Dad. He looked at Kat and sighed. "I wish this pair got along as well as you and Rosie. You're such BFFs!" That was too much for Kat to bear. She was pretty sure that she was in the process of being replaced as Rosie's best friend! She asked if she could leave the table, then she ran upstairs to her room, threw herself on the bed, and started to cry.

Chapter 5
Poachers in the Orchard!

The next day, Kat and Rosie returned to the Lollipop Orchard with Doctor Clarice. They landed the flying carpet near the gingerbread village and started to search the snow for clues. Doctor Clarice had been rehearsing her Gingerbredge—the squeaky language of the gingerbread folk.

While Rosie and Doctor Clarice enthusiastically hunted for mysterious footprints and abandoned nets, Kat trailed behind. She tried to act as if she was helping, but she felt like a fraud. She didn't need to look for clues because she was sure that she knew who the poacher was—Rosie's new friend, Lunella. If only she could tell them!

Suddenly, Rosie gave a shout. "I've found footprints!" Kat rushed over to look. They were very small—too small to have been made by Lunella's boots. Rosie followed the tracks through the snow and under a candy apple bush. "Got you!" she yelled, pulling aside the sugary leaves to reveal … a gummy creature in the shape of a shoe.

"It's a gumshoe," laughed Doctor Clarice. "I don't think that's what we're looking for."

It seemed as though there were no clues anywhere to be found, so Doctor Clarice led the girls to the gingerbread village. Kat was glad they took the long way around the bog this time—it had taken ages to get the sticky toffee out of her boots!

When they got to the village, they were in for a shock. All the gingerbread people were already out in the snow, deep in conversation with a very familiar looking person ...

"Lunella!" gasped Rosie. "What are you doing here?"

Lunella looked just as surprised as Rosie did. "I was asking if they've seen a horse..." she said.

Kat couldn't believe it! She thought of poor Holly, tangled up in the net, and felt hot and angry. "Don't tell her!" she shouted to the mayor. "She's a spy for the Elf King!

She's the one who hurt the flying horse!"

Rosie stared at Lunella in astonishment. "Is this true?" she asked.

"No!" Lunella exclaimed. "Of course not. I would never hurt an animal."

Rosie whirled back to face Kat. "Why would you say something like this?" she asked.

"Because it *is* true," Kat insisted. "I know it is … I read it in her journal!"

A puzzled expression came over Lunella's face and it dawned on Kat what she had blurted out. She was still angry—but now she felt a bit scared too. As she stared down at the snowy ground, she could hear Lunella saying, "I lost my journal in the café."

"You didn't lose it," said Kat miserably. "I took it out of your bag."

Lunella gasped. Out of the corner of her eye, Kat caught sight of Rosie's shocked expression. But before she could explain, Doctor Clarice's crystalzoometer started to make its familiar whizzing sound. At once, all the little gingerbread folk started to squeak excitedly, jumping up and down.

"I'm afraid this is going to have to wait," said Doctor Clarice, looking troubled. "There's an animal nearby that needs our help." She told Kat and Rosie to come with

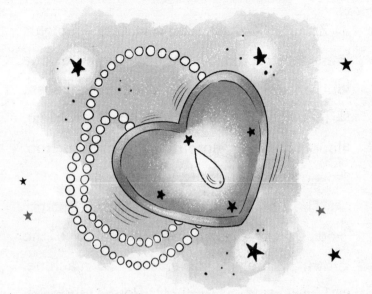

her—and asked Lunella to wait with the gingerbread folk until they came back.

Kat's mind was in a whirl as they crunched through the snow in the direction of the jelly bean caves. Beside her, Rosie looked deep in thought, keeping her eyes on the icy ground. Lunella had been so surprised that it made Kat begin to doubt herself ... Could she *really* be a poacher?

Zzzzub! Zzzzub! Zzzzub! Kat's thoughts were interrupted by the appearance of one of the strangest machines she had ever seen. It looked like a flying bubble with whirling, flapping wings sprouting from the top, hovering over the jelly bean caves.

"That's one of the Elf King's whirlycopters," said Doctor Clarice. She gestured to the crown symbol on the side of the machine. "I know his royal symbol. It looks like we've discovered our poachers."

Inside the machine, two elves were pushing and pulling at the levers that controlled it. Kat saw that they had trapped a green gummy bear in a net. The crystalzoometer stopped whizzing and pointed directly at it. This was what it had been leading them to! There was a shout from the elves, and the whirlycopter jiggled from side to side as

they tried to get into the right position to pick it up. The little bear was struggling to get out, but the sparkling net was too strong. Kat knew that it must be enchanted—just like the magical ropes that had caught poor Holly.

"No!" shouted Doctor Clarice, but there was nothing she could do. The gummy bear gave a wobbly roar as the net swung up into the air, and the whirlycopter flapped away with its precious cargo.

"Don't worry," said Doctor Clarice. "We can follow them on the carpet. Let's collect your friend, then we can get going. " But the flying carpet didn't come when she whistled—and that wasn't all. Lunella was nowhere to be seen either! Eventually, the girls discovered the carpet buried under a huge pile of wet snow. The spinning wings of the whirlycopter had whipped up a small snowstorm that had covered it completely.

"Goodness me!" exclaimed Doctor Clarice.

"We can dig it out." said Rosie, and she
started scooping the soft snow off the buried
carpet.

"I'll help," said Kat. She tried to smile
at Rosie, but her friend wouldn't catch her
eye—even when two helpful honeybunnies
popped up and joined in, using their
strong paws to dig. On any other day, Kat
would have stopped what she was doing to
stroke the cute, furry creatures. Today, she
was too busy worrying about Rosie and
Lunella to pay them much attention.

At last, the carpet was uncovered and
Doctor Clarice examined it carefully.
It looked damp and forlorn. "Oh dear,"
she said sadly. "The engine is wet through!
The carpet won't fly until it's dried out."

Kat shivered. It would be a long, cold walk
back to the surgery in the snow.

Just then, Kat heard the flapping noise of a whirlycopter coming from the other side of the orchard. Surely the elves hadn't come back already? She whipped around to look, but it was a different whirlycopter … with a different driver.

"It's Lunella!" gasped Rosie. "Look at her ears!" Lunella had taken off her hat, and her long, pointy elf ears were plain to see.

"You see," said Kat, as the whirlycopter disappeared into the clouds. "I told you she was the poacher!"

"I can see that she's an *elf*," Rosie said slowly. "But that doesn't mean she's a poacher. Lunella wouldn't do anything to hurt animals."

Kat couldn't believe her ears. "Then why is her journal full of drawings of Holly?" she demanded. As soon as she said it, Rosie's expression changed.

"You shouldn't have read Lunella's journal," she said. "She's our friend."

"She's *your* friend!" said Kat with a sob. Suddenly, all her words came out in a rush. "Now you've got *her*—you don't need *me* anymore!"

Rosie stared at Kat in astonishment. "That's not true," she said.

Kat felt embarrassed. She was very relieved to see Doctor Clarice beckoning them over, holding what looked like three pairs of ice skates.

"I can't get the carpet started, I'm afraid," Doctor Clarice said. "Luckily, I packed the emergency skates."

"Are we going to skate on Rainbow River?" asked Kat, suddenly feeling excited. She loved ice skating. She had spent lots of time skating on the lake with her parents and little brothers.

"Well, I know the river's frozen, but I'm not sure we'd make it over the waterclimb," laughed Doctor Clarice. The waterclimb was a magical waterfall that gushed up instead of down. "Besides, these aren't ice skates— they're snover-skates. Hover skates for snow."

Kat strapped on the skates and found

that she really was hovering just above the ground! It took a moment to get her balance but, as soon as she did, she could see what a wonderful invention they were. Just one tiny push, and she went whizzing along the top of the snow, feeling as light as air.

"These are amazing," said Rosie, giving her an awkward kind of smile. "We'll zoom back to the surgery in no time!"

By the time they reached the surgery, the girls were breathless and rosy-cheeked. Neither of them had mentioned Lunella on the way back. They were both doing their best to act as if nothing had happened, but Kat felt awkward and embarrassed. She had no idea what she could say to make things better.

Doctor Clarice left to talk to Doctor Hart, and the girls went to check on Holly. She was delighted to see the girls and snorted in horsey delight when Rosie fed her another carrot. Her wing seemed to have completely healed.

Doctor Morel had been keeping her company, and he'd brought along some books from the flying library to help. "They like to be around other flying creatures," he said, putting down a book called

A Gnome's Guide to Toadstools and gently swatting away one called *Aquatic Etiquette: How to Behave at a Mermaid's Tea Party.* "I have to check up on the other animals now," he added, "but these books will stay and keep her company." The little books snuggled up in Holly's feathery wings and started to doze off.

Chapter 6

Flying to Cloud Castle

Doctor Hart called an emergency meeting in Doctor Clarice's lab. Doctor Morel was there, and Doctor Clarice of course, and Kat and Rosie were proud to be invited too.

"I think the Elf King is looking for more magical animals for his private zoo," Doctor Hart said sadly. "Holly won't be safe until he moves on—and neither will any of the animals in Starfall Forest."

"Oh my pots and pancakes," muttered Doctor Morel. "He needs a good talking to!"

"Perhaps I could fly up to Cloud Castle

and explain what's happening down here," said Doctor Clarice thoughtfully.

"But the carpet's broken," said Rosie.

Doctor Clarice's eyes twinkled as she crossed the room and pulled on a long, golden rope. A curtain swished to one side, revealing her latest invention—a huge blue balloon, covered in frost, with a basket dangling below it. "It's a cold air balloon," she said proudly. "It runs on snowflakes!" She fiddled with some buttons and a mini blizzard started to whirl furiously inside the balloon. Everyone was very impressed.

Kat asked if they could go with her, but Doctor Clarice shook her head. "The balloon is still at an experimental stage," she said, "and I only have one emergency parachute."

Thrrrrrppp! A funny rasping noise came from the basket and Kat saw a flash of bright orange diving down inside it.

"What was that?" asked Rosie.

Doctor Clarice put a finger up to her lips and tiptoed over to the balloon. Then she peeked over the edge and said, "Boo!"

At once, a little orange animal with a long curly body popped its head over the edge of the basket and playfully stuck out its tongue.

"I thought so!" laughed Doctor Clarice, as the cute creature jumped onto her arm and ran up to her shoulders. "Have either of you met a teasel before?" The girls shook their heads. "Well, we'll need to search the room for another one," she said. "They *always* travel in pairs."

The girls searched the whole room, but there were no other teasels anywhere. It was very strange!

"It looks like this one's coming with me," sighed Doctor Clarice, as the teasel jumped into the cold air balloon, curling itself into loops and snuggling into the pile of cushions. "Never mind! If I have to use the emergency parachute, I can tuck it in my pocket!"

"I wish *we* could come with you," said Kat. Now that the cold air balloon was ready to go, it looked so magical—glimmering with frost and whirring gently. She imagined what it would be like to drift gently up into the sky …

"I'm sorry I can't let you ride in the balloon," said Doctor Clarice. "If only there was another way up to Cloud Castle …"

"There is!" said Rosie breathlessly. "We could ride there on Holly's back! I think she's well enough, but I'll check with Doctor Hart first."

At once, Kat remembered the picture they had seen in the fountain in Rosie's garden. Her eyes shone. Was the vision about to come true at last?

The girls raced through the corridors to Holly's room and found Doctor Hart brushing

Holly's silky mane. "Do you think she's well enough to fly?" Rosie asked.

"I'm sure she is," smiled Doctor Hart. "In fact, I think it would do her good to use her wings again. She's been cooped up inside for quite a while."

"Please can we ride you to Cloud Castle, Holly?" asked Kat gently.

Holly unfurled her wings and whinnied, stamping her foot in excitement.

Rosie and Kat clambered up onto Holly's back, and Doctor Hart led them to a large, moss-covered door in a corner of the room. She pulled a long rope and the door swung open to reveal the cold air balloon hovering in the snowy sky outside. Doctor Clarice waved at them from the basket. The orange teasel was wrapped around her neck like a scarf!

"Are you ready, Rosie?" Kat asked. Her friend gave an excited nod. "Are you ready, Holly?" she whispered.

The horse stamped her foot again, then she started to beat her enormous wings and stepped out into the crisp, cold air. There was a rush of wind and Kat held tightly onto Holly's soft neck. As they soared through the sky, Kat couldn't stop grinning. From this height, all her problems seemed

as small as the sparkling trees in the forest far below. She looked at Rosie and saw that she was grinning too!

"This is incredible!" Kat shouted. She loved the feel of the icy wind, and she felt so safe and secure on Holly's back. Best of all, she was sharing the amazing experience with Rosie. There was no one else she would want to have with her.

The sky around them turned from blue to wispy white, and Kat discovered that they were flying through the clouds. The air felt cold and damp against her face. Up ahead, she saw bright sparkling lights shining from a collection of towers and turrets.

"That must be Cloud Castle!" called Rosie. "Can we go that way, Holly?"

The flying horse beat her strong wings and swooped toward the lights.

The castle sat on an enormous, white cloud studded with rainbow crystals that sparkled with magic. Beside it was the entrance to the Elf King's private zoo. As they drew closer, Kat could hear the roar of a gummy bear, the chattering of birds, and other squeaks, grunts, and howls coming over the high wall that hid the zoo from sight. The zoo was very well guarded. Two elves in smart uniforms were standing to attention on either side of the entrance gate, and several more were patrolling the outside walls.

"Do you think it's safe to land?" Rosie asked nervously.

Then they saw Doctor Clarice waving at them frantically from the cold air balloon ...

"Kat! Rosie!" Doctor Clarice's voice sounded tiny and far away as it floated to them over the clouds. "I'm losing power!" As she spoke, the balloon jiggled from left to right. The teasel jumped off Doctor Clarice's shoulders and dived down into the basket to hide.

"Do you need some help?" hollered Kat.

"I'll be fine," Doctor Clarice called back. "I just need to make an emergency landing!" The girls watched anxiously as Doctor Clarice pulled at the strings to bring the balloon under control. At last, it began to spiral slowly toward the other side of the Elf King's cloud, and she waved cheerfully at the girls. "Tell Holly to land by the castle," she hollered. "I'll meet you there!"

Holly swooped down toward Cloud Castle. Little puffs of white mist flew up into the air as she landed, and she gave a confused neigh. When Kat and Rosie climbed down, they were surprised to find that the cloud was bouncy under their feet. Everything around them seemed to be made of cloud, from the little cloud bushes in rows, to the fluffy flower patches!

The elf guards hadn't seen them land—they were too busy staring at the cold air balloon that was flying above their heads. Kat and Rosie crept closer to hear what they were saying.

"Hey," said the first guard. "I think there's some kind of orange snake flying that balloon."

"A snake?" scoffed her friend. "You must be dreaming."

"Pinch me and see if I wake up!" said the first guard. So her friend reached over and pinched her on the arm.

"Youch!" screeched the first guard, pinching her friend back.

"Owowowow!" shouted her friend. "What did you do that for?"

"You pinched me!"

"You told me to!"

The elves stared at each other crossly, but their fight had alerted the Captain of the Guard.

"Is someone trying to break into the zoo?" he yelled.

At once, the guards stood to attention. "No, Captain!" they chorused. They tried to tell him what they'd seen—but the cold air balloon was long gone.

The more the elf guards explained what they'd seen, the more confused the Captain became! Eventually, he put his hands over his pointy ears. "I've heard enough!" he barked. "Fetch the whirlycopters. If there *is* an orange snake flying a balloon, we can capture it for the Elf King's zoo—and if there *isn't*, then I'm sending both of you off to buy some eyeglasses."

As the whirlycopter flapped up into the sky, Kat looked at the entrance gate and noticed that it was unguarded. "Look!" she whispered to Rosie.

But Rosie wasn't watching the guards any more. She had spotted a flowerbed filled with white feathers and rainbow stones—just like the ones that Lunella had shown them in the café. Sadly, she scooped up a handful of the sparkling stones.

"Rosie!" hissed Kat. "Now's our chance to explore!"

Rosie frowned. "Doctor Clarice told us to meet her by the castle," she said. "Shouldn't we wait for her?"

"Just a quick peek," said Kat.

"Okay," said Rosie, putting the stones in her pocket. "Come on, Holly." The flying horse gave a gentle neigh and trotted after them.

Just outside the gate was an enormous sign that read: "KEEP OUT." Beside it was another one that read: "BY ORDER OF HIS MISTY MAJESTY THE ELF KING." And beside *that* was one that read: "THAT MEANS YOU." The King really didn't want anyone else to visit the animals in his private zoo!

A few white wisps of cloud fluttered toward them and Kat noticed that they had eyes. "I think these are some kind of cloud creatures!" she whispered.

Rosie reached out a hand to stroke one, but it was impossible! Her fingers went straight through it and out the other side. Luckily, it didn't seem to mind at all. She'd never seen anything like it. The funny creatures were just as interested in Kat and Rosie as the girls were in them.

They floated up and down, in their whirly wispy way, blinking and winking as they examined these newcomers from all angles.

"No wonder the Elf King collects other animals," Rosie said. "These little cloud creatures are really cute—but you can't hug them!"

"You can't put them in a zoo either," giggled Kat. "They'd just float out again."

Chapter 7
The Private Zoo

Kat, Rosie, and Holly followed the winding path that led through the zoo. It was very soft underfoot, and even the clip-clop of Holly's hooves was muffled. Each enclosure had a sign that announced each animal's name and where it was from.

The girls stopped by a large enclosure filled with green, leafy trees. "Gummy Bear from Starfall Forest," read Rosie. "Oh! This must be the one that we saw being taken away in the net."

The gummy bear looked up and gave a grumpy growl when it saw them.

"I think it's homesick," said Kat. "Poor bear!" She remembered how upset Holly had been after being caught in an elf net, and stroked the flying horse's soft neck.

"I'm not sure the Elf King knows what gummy bears like best," said Rosie. "They like to sleep in caves made of jelly beans— they don't live in the woods."

"Don't worry, little bear," said Kat. "Doctor Clarice is going to talk to the Elf King. She will sort everything out!"

The girls found themselves walking past signs for creatures that they had never seen before. There were flying fish and shimmering insects and a scaly-looking creature called a crocosmile, which turned and gave them the most enormous, toothy grin! Holly looked alarmed when she saw its sharp teeth.

"Don't worry," said Rosie, patting the horse on her neck. "It's not going to eat you. Look, the zookeeper has left it a big plate of cheese sandwiches."

"It doesn't look very interested in them though," Kat said. "I bet it doesn't eat cheese sandwiches in the wild!"

In the next enclosure, an enormous blue elephant with a trunk in the shape of a trumpet ambled over to greet them. "Hullaballoo from Silvertree Island," read Kat. "I wonder what noise it ..."

Bluuuuuuuuurp! Before she could finish what she was saying, the hullaballoo trumpeted the loudest blast she'd ever heard. Holly gave a surprised whinny and trotted on up the path. The girls put their hands over their ears and followed her.

All the enclosures that the girls passed had creatures in them—except one. Rosie examined the sign. "Boombadger from Starfall Forest," she read out loud. "This creature was returned by order of the King, because of the smell." Kat knew exactly what sort of terrible smell a boombadger could make, so she wasn't surprised.

"I think it's time to go back to the castle," said Kat. They turned to go, but something caught Kat's eye. It was a cage with a furry orange creature curled up in the corner. "It's a teasel!" she said. "Do you remember what Doctor Clarice said? Teasels always travel in pairs—and they can't bear to be apart."

"That's probably why this one looks so unhappy," said Rosie. "I bet its friend is the one we found in Doctor Clarice's balloon!"

Kat nodded. "I'm beginning to think that

the Elf King doesn't know much about animals," she said. "In order to look after them properly, you need to learn everything about them—what they eat, where they live, all the things they like and don't like—but I just don't think he has."

"I agree," said Rosie. "A crocosmile with a cheese sandwich, a gummy bear with no cave, and now a lonely teasel! I wish we could take them all back to the surgery with us!"

"*All* of them?" Kat said.

Holly shook her head and made a snorting, harrumphing noise.

"Holly's saying that she can't fit a hullaballoo on her back," laughed Rosie.

Kat suddenly had an idea. "I know we can't let *all* the animals out," she said excitedly. "But we could take the teasel … And I know just where to find the keys to its enclosure!"

Kat had spotted a small zookeeper's hut nearby. Quietly, she and Rosie led Holly down the path and peeped through the window. Inside, they could see an elf in a zookeeper's uniform—and a large bunch of keys on a table.

"How are we going to get the keys without her noticing?" groaned Rosie.

Kat pressed herself closer to get a better look and was surprised to find that she was slowly sinking into the wall. "I don't believe it!" she gasped. The wall of the hut felt cold and spongey and Kat shivered as she put her arm all the way through it and groped around for the keys. At last, her fingers felt solid metal, and she picked them up, drawing her arm back through the wall as slowly as possible to make sure that the keys didn't clank or jangle.

"Got them!" she hissed triumphantly, and Holly gave a happy neigh.

"Shhh!" hissed Rosie—but it was too late.

"What's that?" said the zookeeper in alarm. "Is there a unicorn outside? Has the pajama-llama escaped? I hope that's not a kelpie I can hear!"

"Quick, hide!" squeaked Rosie.

The girls ducked down behind the hut as the zookeeper came out, but of course, Holly was still in plain sight.

"Well I never," said the zookeeper. "A flying horse! I didn't think that the Elf King had managed to find one of those yet." She seemed entranced by Holly and hadn't noticed Kat and Rosie crouching there, as still as statues. "Hello," she said in a gentle voice. "Don't be scared. I won't hurt you."

Kat could tell that the zookeeper meant what she said. Holly wasn't so sure. She gave an anxious snort and started to back away nervously.

"I'm your friend," said the zookeeper, stepping closer—but that was too much for Holly! With a loud neigh, she stamped her hooves on the floor and unfurled her wings.

"She's going to fly away!" said Rosie in alarm. "Holly, no!"

Kat dropped the bunch of keys and put out her hands to stop Holly, but it was too late. The frightened horse soared up in to the sky and disappeared into the clouds.

The zookeeper snapped out of her trance. "What are you doing here?" she said in a worried voice, staring at Kat and Rosie. "No visitors allowed—by order of the King!"

Just then, a loud fanfare rang out behind them. It sounded like a whole herd of hullaballoos trumpeting at once!

"The King is coming!" squeaked the zookeeper, jumping to attention as the elf trumpeters marched into the zoo. They were followed by an impressive looking figure in flowing purple robes! His long beard

stretched down toward the ground and he was wearing a sparking golden crown. This *had* to be the Elf King.

"Hide!" squeaked Rosie again. This time, the two girls dived for cover behind the nearest bush. They couldn't have picked a worse place! Kat groaned in dismay as the fluffy bush dissolved into wisps of cloud, leaving them crouching at the King's feet.

"Greetings, Your Misty Majesty!" said the zookeeper. "It is a pleasure to see you."

"Yes, yes. Of course it is," snapped the Elf King. "But who is this?"

Kat scrambled to her feet and pulled Rosie up after her. "We're just … er … visitors," she said, wondering if she should bow.

"Visitors?" boomed the King. "I feel a royal tantrum coming on. Nobody visits my zoo but *me*!"

Chapter 8
Lunella's Story

Kat held onto Rosie's hand and gave it a squeeze. Rosie squeezed it back as the trumpet players sounded another fanfare.

"Your Misty Majesty!" announced an elf guard. "You have a visitor."

"*Another* one?" said the Elf King in astonishment. "I didn't even want these two."

But Kat breathed a sigh of relief when she saw that the visitor was none other than Doctor Clarice, with the teasel on her shoulders and Holly trotting safely behind her. Doctor Clarice winked at the girls, then gave a small bow to the King.

The King stared at her. "Have you brought more specimens for my zoo?" he asked. "I've already got one of those orange things, but I've always wanted a flying horse."

"No!" shouted Rosie, rushing over to Holly.

"These aren't specimens," sighed Doctor Clarice. "They're living creatures. And if you've only got *one* teasel, it will be unhappy."

The Elf King looked surprised.

"Is that a crocosmile eating a cheese sandwich I can see over there?" asked Doctor Clarice, shaking her head. "Don't you know that they prefer peanut butter and jelly?"

"I feel a royal headache coming on," said the King, with a frown. "You don't need to tell me why you're here. I can guess! Your plan was to distract me while these two Normilliams stole all my animals!"

"Of course not!" said Doctor Clarice, indignantly.

"Then how do you explain ... this!" demanded the King, pointing to the bunch of keys that Kat had dropped.

"My keys!" gasped the elf zookeeper and darted forward to pick them up. "These open all the enclosures in the zoo."

"I feel a royal arrest coming on!" roared the King, and he stamped his foot on the cloud, sending little puffs of cloud and feathers wafting into the air. A feather landed on his nose and made him sneeze. "Achoo! Guards! Take all my 'visitors' back to Starfall

Forest and leave them in Mazewood," he sniffed. "I'm keeping the flying horse."

Kat looked at Doctor Clarice in alarm. Mazewood was a part of the forest where the trees moved around, making it almost impossible to find your way out. She had nearly gotten lost there once before—and she did not want to go back again!

There was a flurry of wings in the sky above them and a royal whirlycopter twirled down to land beside the zookeeper's hut.

"It's Lunella," gasped Rosie, "and the gingerbread mayor!"

"*Lunella*?" said the Elf King. "What on the clouds is my daughter doing here?"

All eyes turned to look at Lunella as she climbed out of the driver's seat with the little gingerbread man. The Elf King's *daughter*?

Kat could hardly believe it. But she had to admit that Lunella looked every bit the princess in her long elf robes and shining silver tiara.

"How did you find us?" Rosie asked.

"The mayor told me about a flying horse he found trapped in a holly bush," Lunella said. The gingerbread man squeaked excitedly, nodding his head in agreement. "He said that you had rescued her and he showed me the way to Calico Comfrey's surgery. I met Doctor Hart, and she explained where you had gone. I'm so sorry … I came as quickly as I could." Then Lunella caught sight of Holly. She rushed over and threw her arms around the flying horse's neck. "I've been looking everywhere for you!" she said, her voice full of emotion. "I'm so glad you're alright."

For a moment, Kat thought that Holly would back away in fright, just like she had when the zookeeper approached her. But Holly didn't look scared of Lunella at all—in fact, she looked delighted to see the elf princess. The way that she nuzzled her soft nose into Lunella's neck made it clear that she loved and trusted her …

Kat was suddenly sure that there was no way Lunella had ever tried to catch Holly in a net. She had been very wrong.

"How do you know Holly?" she asked in a small voice.

"Holly?" said Lunella, sounding puzzled. "Is that her name?"

Holly gave a happy neigh as if to say that it was, and everyone laughed.

"That's a lovely name for her," Lunella said. "She obviously likes it too! Up to now, I've been calling her 'Harla', which means 'horse' in Elf language."

"I have so many questions," said the Elf King, with a frown.

"So do I," burst out Rosie.

Lunella smiled. "I'm sure you do!" she said, gently stroking Holly's nose. "Let me try to explain!"

"I may be the Elf King's daughter, but I don't agree with everything he does," Lunella said. "I love animals ..."

"I do too," said the King, grumpily.

"Yes, but I don't want to keep them all to myself," said Lunella. "I met Harla—I mean Holly—when Cloud Castle was visiting the Arctic Circle. We became friends, but I never told my father. I knew he would hide her away where nobody else could see her."

Lunella explained that when Holly had taken her flying one day, they had been spotted by the elf guards in their whirlycopters. They knew that the King had always wanted a flying horse and gave chase. They were too far away to see who was on her back!

"I was so scared," Lunella said. "One

of them shot a tangling rope at us, and it got caught on Holly's wing. She started to tumble out of the sky and I slipped off her back! Luckily, the trees broke our fall, but we ended up in different parts of the forest. The guards searched for a while, then gave up and flew away ... But when I looked, I couldn't find Holly either! I've been looking for her ever since."

"It's lucky you weren't hurt!" gasped Rosie.

The Elf King had been listening carefully to the story. He looked worried and upset.

"I feel a royal apology coming on," said the Elf King. "I had no idea that my guards had put you in danger. I have been rather selfish. Thank the clouds you weren't hurt because of it—and thank Holly for keeping you safe."

Lunella smiled and gave Holly a pat. "She's a very special horse," she said.

"I can see that," said the Elf King. "More than that, I can see that she is ... your friend.

Even though she doesn't belong to you, she lets you stroke and ride her."

Doctor Clarice gave a small cough. "There are lots of ways you can be a friend to animals," she said, and she told the King all about the surgery and the amazing things they do—including looking after animals who had escaped from his guards' nets!

The King listened thoughtfully. "I feel a royal announcement coming on," he said. "From now on, my zoo will become more like your surgery. I want to help animals too!" He whispered something to the zookeeper, and she raced over to the teasel's enclosure and unlocked the door.

The little furry creature tumbled out and dashed straight over to its friend, who unwound its long body from Doctor Clarice's neck, squeaking happily.

Chapter 9
Friends Forever!

*L*unella rushed to her father and gave him an enormous hug. All the elf guards cheered.

"What a day!" murmured Doctor Clarice. Then one of the wispy cloud creatures drifted toward her. "What's this?" she asked. "I thought I knew all about magical creatures, but I've *never* seen anything like this before!"

"Oh, there are hundreds of cloud creatures living here," said the Elf King casually. "You may take one home with you for your collection if you wish."

"*Father!*" groaned Lunella, rolling her eyes.

"Thank you, Your Misty Majesty," said

Doctor Clarice, looking amused, "but that's not how we work at Calico Comfrey's."

The Elf King gave a loud chuckle as he thought about what he'd said. "Of course," he said. "I feel another royal announcement coming on. Ahem … The magical rescue vets can visit Cloud Castle whenever they like!" He paused. "Er, can you make it soon?" he added. "It looks like there's a lot I need to learn about how to look after my animals. Perhaps you could teach me?"

Doctor Clarice smiled. "That sounds like a great idea," she said.

The Elf King promised that he would fix the cold air balloon and use it to send all the animals he had taken from the forest back home.

"No more nets?" said Doctor Clarice sternly.

"No more nets," promised the King.

Kat had been listening to everything that was being said, and she knew that she had something to say too. She turned to Lunella. "I'm sorry I took your journal," she said in a small voice. She took the book out of her pocket and handed it over. "And I'm *really* sorry I thought you were a poacher. Er ... Should I be calling you 'Your Misty Majesty'?"

"Well, you could ... " said the elf princess, giving Kat one of her huge grins, "but my friends call me Lunella—and you are

definitely my friend! I can tell from the way that Holly behaves around you. She really trusts you."

Holly stamped her hooves on the ground happily. She seemed delighted that the girls were friends.

Lunella offered to take Doctor Clarice and the gingerbread mayor back to the forest in her whirlycopter while Kat and Rosie rode back with Holly.

"There's one thing I don't understand," said Rosie, as they clambered back onto the flying horse's back. "How could you ever think that I could find someone to replace you as my best friend?"

"Lunella can do so many amazing things," said Kat. "She can whistle and cross her eyes … If I try, I just end up pulling a silly face."

Rosie laughed. "You're my friend because of who you *are*, not what you can *do*!" she said. Then she thought for a moment, and looked serious. "But I think I need to say sorry too. I remember saying that I wished Lunella was with us when you couldn't whistle—and when you didn't laugh at the back-to-front bird. I'm sorry, that must have hurt your feelings."

Kat nodded, and the girls hugged each other.

"Best friends forever," said Rosie.

When the girls arrived back at the surgery,
Lunella was waiting outside in the snow
with Doctor Hart. "I'm so pleased about
the Elf King's change of heart," the kindly
woman beamed. "It's more than I ever
dreamed would happen!"

Lunella smiled. "Doctor Hart wants to
give Holly one last check-up," she said.
"Then I'm going to take her back home to
the Arctic."

"Would you like a hot chocolate before
you go?" Kat asked shyly.

"Yes, please," said Lunella happily.
"Just give me a moment to hide my ears!"

In the café, the girls ordered three hot
chocolates with extra marshmallows, and
Rosie took out the rainbow stones she had
picked up earlier. "Perhaps we can make
another snowman tomorrow," she said.

"Oh!" said Lunella. "I would love to, but I'm afraid we won't be here tomorrow. Cloud Castle never stays anywhere for long. We're always on the move."

Rosie looked sad, and Kat found that she felt sad too.

"I'll write you letters," promised Lunella. "We'll be busy for a while, returning the animals to their homes. But I'll visit whenever we pass over Starfall Forest."

"I'm going to miss you," said Kat—and she really meant it.

A cold wind started to blow as the girls left the café. To their delight, a flurry of snowflakes started to fall from the sky, and they all stuck out their tongues to see if they could catch any.

"I've got one!" shouted Lunella.

"Me too!" giggled Kat.

Starfall Forest looked even more magical than ever as the snow settled on the bare branches of the trees, making them glisten and glow.

"Can we have a last ride on Holly before you go?" asked Rosie as they reached the surgery.

"You'll have to ask her," said Lunella—but Holly was already unfolding her enormous white wings.

"I think that's a yes," said Lunella, laughing.

Kat and Rosie climbed on Holly's back,

and the flying horse soared up into the sky above Starfall Forest. Snowflakes danced and twinkled in the air around them, and Lunella glided and looped alongside them in her whirlycopter.

"Thank you, Holly," whispered Kat, nuzzling the horse's warm neck. She felt like the luckiest girl alive as she zoomed through the wintry sky with her three amazing friends!

Starfall Forest Map